IZZY

THE INVISIBLE

Izzy
THE INVISIBLE

by Louise Gray

illustrated by
Laura Ellen Anderson

Piccadilly
PRESS

First published in the UK in 2016
by Piccadilly Press
80-81 Wimpole St, London W1G 9RE
www.piccadillypress.co.uk

Text copyright © Jim Eldridge 2016
Illustrations copyright © Laura Ellen Anderson 2016

ISBN: 978-1-848-12509-4
also available as an ebook

3 5 7 9 10 8 6 4
Designed by Tracey Cunnell
Printed and bound by Clays Ltd, St Ives Plc

Piccadilly Press is an imprint of Bonnier Publishing Fiction,
a Bonnier Publishing company
www.bonnierpublishingfiction.co.uk

For Lynne,
for ever
LG

For Phil and Alicia.
Two very wonderful
and supportive people
in my life xxx
LEA

CHAPTER 1:
How it All Began

"Breakfast!"

Seven-year-old Izzy Clark heard her mum calling from the kitchen and reluctantly switched off *Pet Club*, her favourite TV programme that she watched every Saturday morning. It featured all sorts of great animals.

Izzy would love to have a pet, but Mum and Dad didn't want one. Izzy liked dogs and cats, but she *really* loved unusual pets.

I'd love a pet like Pete the Talking Parrot on Pet Club, thought Izzy as she walked along the hall.

Luckily for Izzy, her grandmother had LOADS of pets that she could visit and play with. Nana Lin had two dogs, three cats, a snake and a parrot called Perky who flew around her house. Perky could even talk! Not as well as Pete, but enough to have fun confusing Nana's dogs and cats by talking to them in a mixture of voices. Perky was brilliant!

"Breakfast!" Mum called again, louder this time.

"Here I am," replied Izzy from the kitchen doorway.

"Can you tell Carrie and your dad to hurry up, please?" Mum said as she put muesli and cereal boxes, tubs of yoghurt and toast on the table. "I've got to get to work."

Izzy headed upstairs. On her big sister's bedroom door hung a handwritten sign. It said:

Izzy opened the door. "Carrie . . ." she began.

"Can't you read?!" her sister snapped, pointing at the sign.

"That's why I came in," said Izzy. "To ask permission."

Carrie sighed. "You're supposed to knock first."

This was an argument the two sisters had most days.

"But it doesn't say that on the sign," pointed out Izzy.

Carrie closed the diary she'd been writing in. It was a small notebook with pictures of her favourite pop stars on the cover. Carefully she wrapped a ribbon around it, then tied it in a neat bow before placing it in the drawer of her dressing table.

"What are you writing?" Izzy asked. She was a very curious girl, and always asking questions.

5

"None of your business," answered Carrie.

"Were you writing about me?" asked Izzy.

Carrie frowned. "Why would I write about you?" she said. "Anyway, what do you want?"

"Mum says that breakfast is ready," Izzy told her.

Izzy wandered over to where her older sister's make-up was spread out on her dressing table: bottles of different coloured nail polish and jars of glitter stars.

"I like this one," said Izzy, picking up a small purple bottle.

"Don't touch that!" squealed Carrie, making Izzy jump.

But Izzy had already taken off the lid and at that moment she dropped the tiny bottle, spilling purple liquid on the tabletop.

"Now look what you've done!" shouted Carrie, upset. "You're so clumsy!"

"What's going on?" called Mum from downstairs.

"Izzy's messed up my stuff!" Carrie yelled. "She's spilled nail polish everywhere!"

"You can both clean it up later!" Mum shouted back. "Breakfast is ready, and I have to go to work!"

"I've got to clean it before it stains!"

"I'll help you," offered Izzy.

Carrie glared at Izzy. "No you won't, you'll just make it worse! Keep your hands off my stuff."

Izzy sniffed. She hadn't meant to make a mess, but it was bound to happen sometimes when you were a little bit clumsy and very curious. And it wasn't all her fault, Izzy thought, Carrie had made her jump by shouting so loudly.

As she hurried out of Carrie's room, Izzy bumped into Dad.

"Hey, what's all the shouting about?" he asked.

"Nothing," replied Izzy quickly. "Breakfast is ready."

Izzy walked downstairs with Dad and joined Mum in the kitchen.

"I thought *you* were going to prepare breakfast today," Mum said accusingly to Dad. "I've got to get ready for work."

"I was stuck on the phone," Dad explained.

"You're always stuck on the phone," Mum pointed out.

"Yes, but this was an emergency," groaned Dad. "We've got a problem with the hot water at the gym. I've got to go in and meet the plumber to sort it out."

Mum glared at him.

"But you said you'd look after Izzy

today!" she said. "It's Saturday — I've got appointments booked!"

Mum ran her own hair and beauty salon called Fresh Cutz, and Dad was the manager at the local health club and gym.

"I'm sorry," apologised Dad. "But I've got to go in, I'm the manager!"

As Carrie came into the kitchen, Mum asked her, "Can you look after Izzy today?"

Carrie sat down at the table and shook her head.

"No way," she said. "I'm going to Vicky's, and there's no way I'm taking Izzy. She'd probably mess things up and Vicky wouldn't talk to me again!"

"That's not a very nice thing to say about your sister," Dad said disapprovingly.

Carrie didn't reply, but it was obvious from her expression that she wasn't sorry.

Huh, thought Izzy, feeling annoyed.

They're talking about me as if I'm not even here! I might as well be invisible! Then she had an idea.

"I could go to Nana Lin's," she suggested hopefully.

Mum hesitated, then sighed and reached for her phone.

CHAPTER 2

Nana Lin's

"I love going to Nana's!" said Izzy as she and Mum walked to the car.

"Hmm," said Mum. "The trouble is you're always in such a mess when you come back. Dog hairs. Cat hairs. Feathers! And not to mention her experiments!"

Nana Lin was a retired science teacher, but she still carried out experiments — in her kitchen! Most of them involved a lot of mess and some very odd smells (just like her cooking).

"Nana is even more messy than you, Izzy," said Mum.

Izzy remembered the spilled nail polish in Carrie's room and felt bad. As they reached the car, Izzy saw their next-door neighbour, Mrs Rice, glaring at them from her front garden.

"What's wrong with Mrs Rice?" whispered Izzy. "She looks really angry about something."

"Someone broke into her garden and made a mess of it," said Mum.

"Does she think it was me?" asked Izzy, horrified. "Because she's looking at me in a really bad way."

"She's just upset," said Mum. "Come on, get in the car."

☆ ° ◎ ☆ ° ☆

Nana Lin's house was a bungalow surrounded by an overgrown garden filled with trees and wild flowers. Mum was always offering to neaten it up and "at least trim the hedges", but Nana Lin insisted that she liked it just as it was.

"This garden's like me," she said. "Old, happy . . . and a little wild."

"Messy, more like," Mum added under her breath.

To Izzy, her nana's house and garden were magical places where exciting things happened.

As they parked outside Nana Lin's house, there was the sound of a small explosion from inside, followed by dogs barking and a strange squawking, which

Izzy knew was Perky the parrot.

"Oh no," groaned Mum. "I hope she hasn't done anything silly!"

The front door of the house opened and smoke poured out, along with two cats: Itsy, a tabby, and Bitsy, who was ginger. As Izzy watched, the cats climbed rapidly up the trunk of the apple tree and perched themselves on one of the branches. They didn't look very impressed – not one bit.

As Izzy walked up the path, Nana Lin's two dogs, Griff (a small black-and-white terrier) and Gruff (a very large, very floppy, red-haired dog) also rushed out of the house. Izzy laughed as they began to leap about to say hello, barking excitedly and licking her face and hands.

It tickled! Then she spotted her nana who was beaming at them, a cloud of grey smoke hanging around her head.

"There you are!" she called.

"Hi, Nana!" Izzy said happily.

"We heard an explosion," Mum said, a bit unhappily.

"It wasn't really an explosion," said Nana Lin. "More of a . . . *pop!*"

"A very *loud* 'pop'," muttered Mum, frowning.

"Nothing serious," said Nana Lin. "But it's set the animals off. Do you want a cup of tea?"

"I can't stop," said Mum. "I've got a client due." She kissed Izzy goodbye. "I'll see you later, darling. Be good!"

With that, Mum headed back down

the path through the front garden towards her car.

"Right," said Nana to Izzy. "Come through and I'll show you what I'm doing."

Izzy hurried after Nana to the kitchen, closely followed by Griff and Gruff.

Nana's kitchen was amazing. It looked chaotic. To one side, on a worktop, was a glass tank filled with rocks and sand, where Sid — Nana Lin's pet snake — lived. Every other surface in the kitchen was covered with jars, pots, saucepans and cooking equipment, and every shelf was stacked with packets and tubs and bottles. Many of these didn't have labels, but Nana claimed she knew what was in absolutely everything.

The only free spaces in the room were the top shelves of the kitchen cabinets, and so these were where Nana's cats liked to sit, watching the activity below. Buddy, the third of Nana's cats, was crouching on a shelf right now, looking down very suspiciously towards the cooker.

Izzy noticed
that smoke was
rising from an
empty saucepan on the hob
and there was a puddle of liquid
on the floor below it. Griff and Gruff
rushed through and began licking it up.

"Good dogs!" said Nana.

Izzy looked warily at them
licking the puddle.

"Are you sure it's all right
for them to eat one of your
experiments?" she asked.
"Isn't it chemicals or
something?"

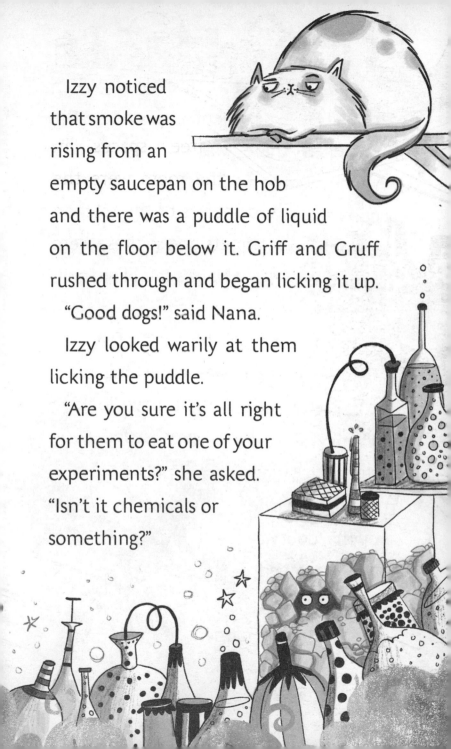

"No," said Nana. "It's soup! When my latest experiment exploded in the saucepan there was a huge BANG! which made me jump and I spilt my cup of soup."

Nana bent down to pick up a cup that had rolled under the table, and put it in the sink.

"Izzy! Izzy!" called a familiar parrot voice.

Izzy grinned happily as Perky the parrot flew in through the open doorway and perched on her head, squawking her name.

"Hello, Perky!" she greeted the parrot.

"Oh, Perky loves it when you come round," said Nana, smiling. He certainly seemed to enjoy his new perch!

"What's happened to Sid?" asked Izzy, peering into the glass tank. All she could see was sand and rocks, with no sign of the snake.

"Looks like he's gone into hiding," said Nana. "I think the bang scared him."

Nana tapped on the side of the glass and Sid's head peered out from beneath a pile of small rocks. At first it was difficult to see him, because Sid's skin was the same colour as the sand. He was camouflaged. The snake peered around, and then withdrew back behind the rocks.

"I think he's going back to sleep," said Nana. "Snakes are such lazy creatures!"

And not very cuddly, thought Izzy.

Proudly, Nana pointed at the saucepan, which was still smoking. "Anyway, this is my latest experiment: Vanishoo!"

"Vanishoo?" repeated Izzy, puzzled.

"It makes things disappear," said Nana.

"Why would you want to make things disappear?" Izzy asked.

"Think about it!" said Nana excitedly. "Unsightly rubbish, making everything look messy. Vanishoo will sort it out!"

Izzy had to smile at this. Nana was the messiest person she knew.

"No more litter, bills or letters from the council."

Nana always seemed to be in trouble with the local council over things like her overgrown front hedge, or parking her car in the wrong place.

"But the mess would still be there, you just wouldn't be able to see it," pointed out Izzy.

"Yes, true, and that's the next part of it I need to work on," said Nana. She frowned. "Right now I'm having trouble with the first bit, getting stuff to vanish. There's obviously something missing from the mixture."

Nana headed to a cupboard and began

rummaging around inside it, while Izzy approached the saucepan and peered into it. A blue-ish gloop was bubbling away at the bottom of the saucepan.

"How do you make Vanishoo?" asked Izzy, turning back to Nana. As she turned, her arm knocked over a bottle next to the cooker. The bottle fell on its side, rolling towards the hob and, before Izzy could stop it, some of the liquid inside splashed into the saucepan.

The blue gloop bubbled violently, and sent up a small, fluffy dark blue cloud that made Izzy sneeze! It also made her feel tingly all over.

"Yuck!" said Izzy. "This stuff's awful!"

"Yuck!" squawked Perky, flying off Izzy's head and joining Buddy on the top of the kitchen shelf.

The cat and parrot were old friends, and they sat together watching Izzy intently. Then Griff and Gruff began barking frantically at her.

"Shush!" ordered Nana.

The dogs obediently stopped barking, but they still kept their eyes fixed on Izzy as if there was something wrong.

All I did was sneeze, thought Izzy.

Nana came out of the cupboard. She frowned. "Izzy?" she called, looking around the kitchen.

"I said this stuff in the saucepan is awful!" said Izzy. "It went up my nose and it's horrible!"

Nana looked around the kitchen suspiciously.

"Izzy!" she said sternly. "I can hear you talking. This is no time for jokes. Come out, wherever you are!"

Izzy looked at Nana, puzzled. It was strange – Nana wasn't actually looking at

Izzy, instead she was looking around the kitchen as if searching for something.

"What do you mean?" asked Izzy.

"Izzy!" squawked Perky, and flew down from the kitchen shelf to land on Izzy's head again.

"AAAARGH!!!" screamed Nana and she stumbled back against the table.

Immediately the two dogs started barking again.

Holding her nose with one hand, Nana rushed to the cooker and slammed a lid firmly down on the saucepan with the blue gloop in it.

"Quiet, Griff! Quiet, Gruff!" Nana ordered firmly. She looked intently at Izzy, a worried expression on her face. Then she said, "Perky! Get off Izzy!"

The parrot obeyed, lifting up into the air, and as it did so Nana let out an unhappy cry. "Oh no! I don't believe it!"

"What's the matter?" asked Izzy.

Nana was behaving very oddly – even for Nana!

"Look in the mirror, Izzy, and see for yourself!" said her grandmother.

Izzy walked over to the large mirror on the wall next to Sid's tank, and looked into it. But all she could see reflected in the mirror was the kitchen, and her Nana, looking worried. She couldn't see her own reflection.

"Where am I?" asked Izzy, bewildered.

And then the truth hit her.

"I'm invisible!" she gasped.

CHAPTER 3:
Invisible Izzy

"Perky, fly back to Izzy," ordered Nana.

Once again, the parrot flew down. As he landed on her shoulder, Izzy felt the tingling sensation again and saw her reflection appear in the mirror.

"What's going on?" asked Izzy.

Nana looked at the fallen bottle lying beside the saucepan.

"This must have spilled into the mixture!" she said, carefully picking it up. "It must be the missing ingredient for my Vanishoo!"

"But why do I appear again when Perky lands on me?" asked Izzy.

"I don't know," admitted Nana. "It must be some sort of chemical reaction. Was Perky with you when the bottle spilled into the mixture?"

"Yes, he was sitting on my head," explained Izzy. "There was a puff of blue smoke and it made me sneeze."

"Ah. That's the reason, then," said Nana. "He's linked to the chemical reaction."

"But he must have breathed in the smoke too. Why doesn't Perky become invisible?" wondered Izzy.

"He's a parrot! Bird biology is very different," said Nana.

"But I can't have Perky perched on my head for the rest of my life!" said Izzy, upset. What would she do at school in PE and Drama? Izzy loved Perky very much, but she felt a bit worried at the idea of being invisible without him. And she couldn't imagine sleeping in bed with a parrot on her head!

"Well, let's see. I have an idea . . ." said Nana. She reached out and plucked a feather from Perky, making him squawk and fly into the air. As soon as Perky left her shoulder, Izzy felt the tingle and she vanished again.

Griff and Gruff barked once, then fell silent and looked at her suspiciously.

Can they see me, or can they just smell me? thought Izzy. She felt quite hopeless suddenly.

But as Nana reached out and touched Izzy with the feather, Izzy felt that same tingle and saw her body reappear in the mirror.

"There," said Nana, handing Izzy the feather.

"You mean I have to hold a feather in my hand all the time?" asked Izzy. She was pleased that Nana could see her again, but she was still a bit worried. Holding on to a feather would be a bit of a pain.

"Try putting it in your pocket," suggested Nana. "It should still work because it's touching you."

Izzy did, and was hugely relieved to find that she stayed visible!

"Good," said Nana. "That'll keep you from vanishing while I work out how to solve this problem. Your mum won't be happy if you're still turning invisible when she comes to collect you!"

For the rest of the day, Nana tried to find a cure, a potion that would stop Izzy from being invisible. Izzy sat on a stool in the kitchen and watched her for a while, but she soon got bored. All that Nana seemed to be creating were huge clouds of smoke from boiling saucepans and smouldering test tubes, and lots of very nasty smells.

So Izzy went out into the garden to amuse herself by playing Hide and Seek with Griff and Gruff, while Itsy and Bitsy watched from the apple tree. When Izzy tried to fool the two dogs by taking the feather out of her pocket and vanishing, the two cats stood up on the branch and yowled loudly, their fur bristling. Nana came outside to see why the animals were making such a row, but she couldn't see invisible Izzy.

The two dogs soon found her by sniffing around the garden, but when Perky flew outside after Nana, he seemed to be the only one who knew instantly exactly where Izzy was. Because of their connection, Perky could see Izzy even when she was invisible! He swooped down to land on her shoulder, making Izzy reappear.

"What are you up to?" demanded Nana. "You're upsetting the animals. All that row they're making will have the neighbours complaining."

"I was just playing Hide and Seek," said Izzy, putting the feather back in her pocket. "But I'm sure the animals know

I'm there even when I'm invisible."

"That's because animals have a sixth sense," said Nana.

"What's a sixth sense?" asked Izzy.

"It means they can see, hear and smell things that we humans can't. Like they can hear some sounds that are too high or too low for the human ear." Nana glanced warily towards the houses that overlooked her garden. "I hope you haven't been making yourself invisible out here, where the neighbours can see what's going on?"

"Er . . . Only a little bit," said Izzy.

"You have to be careful, Izzy," said Nana. "You'd better come inside now. At least no one will see you when you're inside the house."

"No one can see me when I'm outside, either," joked Izzy, following Nana into the house with Griff and Gruff hurrying in after her. The two cats stayed up the tree, watching Izzy suspiciously. They were obviously having nothing to do with this girl who kept appearing and disappearing.

"Actually, I don't mind being invisible," said Izzy.

She smiled to herself at the thought of the fun she could have. She could go to places where she wasn't allowed and no one would know! She could stand right next to people and listen to what they were saying and discover their secrets! And she could scare people by pretending to be a ghost and making things move around in the air.

Nana looked at the mess in her kitchen, at the various mixtures she'd already experimented with, and the many bottles still to try. "I'm going to find the answer to this!" she said with determination.

But Izzy could tell that her grandmother was very worried.

By the end of the afternoon, Izzy was still invisible — unless she had Perky's feather in her pocket. When the doorbell rang Izzy went to let her mum in while her worried-looking nana carried on with her experiments in the kitchen.

"What a terrible day I've had!" sighed Mum as she came into the hall. "Everything went wrong. Sharon didn't come in because she was ill, so I had no assistant. One of the hairdryers packed up. And two clients didn't show up for their appointments!" She gave a long sigh. "How's your day been with Nana?"

"I turned invisible," she said.

"Really, Izzy!" Mum ticked her off. "Talk sensibly."

"I did. . . Look."

Izzy took the feather out of her pocket and put it on the hall table.

"AAAAARGHH!!!!" said Mum, before she fainted.

Nana came hurrying from the kitchen and saw Mum lying on the floor.

"What happened?" she asked.

Izzy picked up the feather, put it in her pocket, and reappeared.

"I think she had a shock," she said.

CHAPTER 4:

The Secret in the Cupboard

Nana had insisted that they take Perky home with them, in case they needed another feather.

"Perky won't mind," Nana told them. "Just pluck a feather from him. He's got lots. And he's moulting, so it won't hurt."

But Perky was the least of Mum's worries. Her hands were still shaking on the steering wheel as she drove home with Izzy and the parrot in the back.

"I can't believe it!" she said, horrified. "Invisible!"

Carrie was in the kitchen making herself a snack when Mum and Izzy arrived home.

"Dad phoned," she said. "He's still stuck at work." She saw Perky and frowned. "Why have you got Perky with you?"

"In case I lose his feather from my pocket," said Izzy, pulling it out to show her sister.

"What do you need one of Perky's feathers for?" asked Carrie.

Izzy put it down on the worktop. She felt the tingling sensation again, and vanished.

Carrie stared at the empty space where Izzy had been standing, her eyes goggling.

Izzy picked up the feather and became visible again.

"That is so cool!" said Carrie, in awe.

"It is not 'cool'!" snapped Mum. "It's . . . awful!"

"What happened?" asked Carrie.

"Some experiment of your Nana Lin's," Mum told her. "It went wrong and Izzy got mixed up in it! Nana said she's going to find a way to stop it happening. Until she does, Perky stays with us."

"Perky and Izzy! Perky and Izzy!" squawked Perky, flying around the inside of the house and coming to land on the banisters.

"Izzy's so lucky!" said Carrie jealously. "Can I have a pet, too?"

"Perky is not Izzy's pet!" said Mum. "He's only with us while this . . . terrible thing is going on."

"I don't think it's terrible," Izzy whispered to her sister. "I think being invisible is wonderful!"

Carrie flashed her a secret smile.

Mum was frowning. "Drat!" she said, annoyed.

"What is it?" asked Carrie.

"I left something in the car."

A few minutes later Mum returned carrying something that looked like a large shoe box with patterns on the outside.

"What's that?" Izzy asked.

"It's a surprise," said Mum. She put it in the cupboard. "And I don't want you girls touching it. So leave it alone."

With that, Mum went upstairs to change out of her salon clothes, while Carrie took her snack into the living room.

Izzy looked at the cupboard with the mysterious cardboard box inside it.

"What do you think's in that box, Perky?" she asked the parrot.

"Box!" repeated Perky. "Box, box!"

"Exactly," nodded Izzy. "There's only one way to find out."

Izzy walked over to the cupboard, but as she took hold of the door handle, Perky screeched, "Leave it! Leave it!"

He was imitating Mum's instruction.

"Sssh!" Izzy warned Perky. She shot a look towards the door. No one was coming.

"Leave it!" squawked Perky again.

"Traitor," Izzy grumbled, giving in.

Then an idea struck her, making her smile. It was time to put her invisibility to the test and have some fun with it!

Izzy took the feather out of her pocket and put it safely on the kitchen unit, then shooed Perky off her shoulder. She felt the now familiar tingle of invisibility and a flutter of excitement, too. Then, with Perky flying behind her, Izzy crept into the living room where Carrie was reading a magazine.

Izzy carefully picked up the small plate that Carrie had left on the coffee table and lifted it up in the air, waving it about.

"Argh!" cried Carrie, momentarily startled, then she scowled. "Stop that, Izzy!" she scolded.

"It's not me. I am a ghost," whispered Izzy, and she let out a long, drawn-out moan: "Whoooooo-ooooo."

"Mum! Izzy's being invisible!" called out Carrie.

"Izzy! Stop doing that!" called Mum from upstairs.

Izzy put the plate back down on the coffee table.

"Huh!" she snorted, annoyed.

With Perky flying after her, she headed for the kitchen.

"This is no fun, Perky," she grumbled. "Being invisible should be fun, don't you think?"

"Box!" squawked the parrot.

Izzy looked at the cupboard.

One little peek can't do any harm, she thought. *Just to find out what it is. After all, that's why secrets exist — so people can find out what they are.*

She started towards the cupboard, but even though Izzy was invisible, Perky could still see her, of course. Once again he squawked a warning, "Leave it!" but before he could repeat himself, Izzy tapped his beak and gave him a serious look.

"It's only a peek, Perky," she whispered. "I'm not doing anything wrong."

Perky seemed to shake his head as if to say *Yes, you are*, but Izzy wasn't paying attention.

"This is where being invisible comes in useful," she added.

Perky gave up and perched on the back of a chair, watching Izzy disapprovingly.

She opened the cupboard and lifted the lid off the cardboard box. Inside was a cake. And not just any cake – this one had a covering made of chocolate and marzipan. Marzipan was Izzy's all-time favourite!

"Wow!" whispered invisible Izzy.

CHAPTER 5:

The Icing on the Cake

The cake was beautiful. Half of the topping was dark chocolate — Carrie's favourite — and the other half was marzipan. It was a dream come true.

I'll just have a little taste, thought Izzy. *Just a tiny piece, so small that no one will notice.*

She picked off a tiny piece of marzipan from the very bottom of the cake and popped it into her mouth. Mmmm, it was delicious!

Maybe just one more piece, she thought. *One tiny piece more.*

She picked another bit off, slightly bigger this time. And that was delicious, too. Marzipan really was Izzy's favourite treat!

She was just picking off another piece when she heard a noise from the hallway. Izzy jumped away from the open cupboard. As her mum came in, she spotted the cake. There were three holes in the topping – it didn't look special or fancy at all any more.

"Oh no! Perky!" exclaimed Mum.

"Perky!" echoed the parrot, still perched on the chair right next to the open cupboard.

"You are a very bad parrot!" said

Mum, obviously upset. "That cake was a surprise for Carrie and Izzy, and now you've ruined it!"

Mum strode over to Perky and waggled her finger at him.

"I'm taking you back to Nana Lin's, and I'm never going to let you come back here again, because I can't trust you. You are a very, very bad parrot!"

Perky flew up onto Mum's arm obediently. As Izzy watched, she felt a rush of sadness. The cake had been a surprise, and she'd ruined it. Worse still, she'd got Perky in trouble when it wasn't his fault. Now he was going to be banned from the house for ever.

"No, Mum!" Izzy burst out, and she snatched up the feather.

Mum looked at Izzy, shocked, as she reappeared in front of her.

"Izzy!" she said. "I didn't know you were in here."

"It was me," admitted Izzy, shamefaced. "I picked at the cake, not Perky. I didn't mean to, I was just curious about what was inside the box. And when I opened it and saw the marzipan . . ." She hung her head in shame.

"And you turned invisible so that I wouldn't see you?" asked Mum grimly. "That was very sneaky, Izzy. You used your invisibility because you knew that what you were doing was wrong." She looked at Perky who had flown onto the table. "Because of that you got Perky into big trouble."

"I know," said Izzy, almost in tears. "I'm so sorry."

Mum walked over to the table and stroked Perky's feathers. "But you owned up," she said. "That was a brave thing to do, Izzy. It shows you have a good heart." She opened her arms to give Izzy a hug, and after a minute she sighed. "Izzy, you have to act properly even though you're invisible. I'm not happy it's happened, but it has, and until Nana Lin comes up with a cure we have to learn to live with it. And that means you need to make responsible decisions. You can't use your invisibility just because *you* think it's fun, or to do things that you know are wrong. It's not fair to other people. It's not right."

Mum bent down and looked into Izzy's eyes.

"I think it's best if you don't turn invisible any more, Izzy. Who knows, the next time you might even stay invisible for ever? I love you so much and I want you to be happy and have fun, but from now on, no more being invisible. Keep Perky's feather on you at all times, okay? Promise?"

"I promise," said Izzy.

Then Mum let out a groan. "Except to show Dad what's happened when he comes in, of course. He won't believe us otherwise!"

☆ ○ ◎ ☆ ○ ☆

Dad was staring at the empty space where his youngest daughter had been standing a second ago. His eyes were wide with shock.

"What-what-what-what...?" he gabbled.

Mum handed back the feather to Izzy, and she reappeared.

"What-what . . . what happened?" asked Dad, still staring goggle-eyed and stunned at his youngest daughter.

"Some experiment of your mother's," Mum told him. "It went wrong!"

"It wasn't all Nana's fault. I might have splashed some stuff into the mixture she was making," Izzy admitted, adding quickly, "by accident."

"We have to take Izzy to a doctor," said Dad.

"We can't," Mum told him. "If we do,

it could get your mother in trouble. Anyway, she said she's going to find a way to stop it happening."

"When?" asked Dad.

"As soon as she can," said Mum.

With trembling fingers, Dad took out his phone and called Nana.

"Mum," he said, "I've just seen Izzy. Or, rather, I haven't seen her. She's invisible!"

Izzy and Mum could just hear Nana Lin's muffled voice through the telephone as she explained what had happened.

"How soon will you come up with a cure?" begged Dad when she'd stopped talking. He listened again and then hung up.

"What did she say?" asked Mum.

"She told me to let her get on," Dad said. "She said, 'I won't find it if you keep phoning me up all the time and interrupting me!'"

☆ ｡ ◎ ☆ ｡ ☆

But Dad wasn't the type to let things go. He made three more phone calls to Nana that evening, and the first thing he did when he got up the next morning was to call her again.

"Any news?" he asked his mother as the family sat down for breakfast.

"No!" barked Nana down the phone. "I keep

No!

telling you, leave me alone so I can work on it! It's Sunday and it's sunny.

Why don't you get outside and do something to take your mind off Izzy's invisibility?"

Dad hung up and looked miserably at the rest of the family.

"She hasn't had any luck yet," he told them. "She says we ought to try and take our minds off it."

"That might be a good idea," said Mum. "If we just hang around the house waiting for Nana to call it will be a miserable day. And she's got our mobile numbers if she makes a breakthrough."

"Can we go to the park?" asked Izzy. "I haven't played with my Frisbee for ages!"

"Well, I'm not playing with you," said Carrie. "It is *so* uncool!"

Izzy slumped in her seat, disappointed.

"Your dad can play Frisbee with you," said Mum. "Carrie and I can check out La Claire, that new boutique on the High Street. It's having a special opening today. What do you think, Carrie?"

"Yes!" smiled Carrie happily.

"Great!" said Izzy. "I'll fetch Perky."

"We can't take Perky to the park," Dad told her. "What if he flies off?"

"He wouldn't, I know he wouldn't," protested Izzy. "And people take dogs," she pointed out.

"Yes, but dogs have to be kept on a lead. You can't keep a parrot on a lead. I'm pretty sure there's a law against parrots in parks," Dad replied.

"A law against parrots?" Izzy was stumped. It was her first morning with Perky and she had to leave him behind. What rotten luck!

Izzy trudged unhappily upstairs to her room to collect her Frisbee. Perky was perched on the end of her bed, and as she came in he flew up and settled on her shoulder.

"We're going out, Perky," said Izzy sadly. "But you can't come with us because of some silly law about parrots."

"Squawk! Law?" squawked Perky.

"Yes, it is a very silly and squawky law," nodded Izzy. "But it's only for a few hours, then we'll be back. Will you be all right while I'm gone?"

"All right! All right!" echoed Perky.

He flew off Izzy's shoulder and perched on the end of her bed again.

"I'll see you later, Perky," said Izzy as she left with the Frisbee. "Be good."

A moment later, as Izzy was walking down the stairs, Perky flew to the window, used his beak to open it and flew outside. He was an exceptionally clever parrot. He settled down on the roof and watched Mum, Dad, Carrie and Izzy leave the house.

☆ ∘ ◎ ☆ ∘ ☆

As they headed for the car, Izzy saw Mrs Rice glaring at them from her window.

"Mrs Rice is so scary!" shuddered Izzy.

"She's just upset," said Dad.

To their surprise, Dad opened Mrs Rice's garden gate, walked up to her front door and rang the bell. There was a pause, then the door opened and Mrs Rice looked out at Dad suspiciously. He started talking, and although Izzy and Carrie and Mum couldn't hear what he was saying, it was obviously something nice, because she gave a nod.

Dad rejoined them, and they made for the car.

"What was that about?" asked Mum.

"I just wanted to tell her that if there was anything we could do to help, all she had to do was ask."

"That's really lovely of you," smiled Mum.

"Why is she so upset?" asked Izzy, curious.

"Someone got into her front garden and made a really bad mess of it," said Dad.

"Remember, I told you, Izzy," said Mum.

"What did they do?" asked Izzy. "Did they damage her plants?"

"More than that," said Dad. "You know those fancy glass ornaments hanging in her apple tree as wind chimes, the ones that made really lovely sounds when the wind blew?"

"Oh yes!" said Izzy. "They were pretty."

"Well, the vandals ripped them down and smashed them. That's why she's upset and always watching out now — she's worried they'll come back and do more damage."

"That's terrible!" said Carrie, looking sad.

And then an idea struck Izzy! Trying to keep the eagerness out of her voice, she said, as casually as she could, "Hey, I've got an idea — why don't we call in at Mr Khan's gift shop on the way?

He's always got interesting stuff to look at."

"That's a good idea!" said Mum. "I'm planning to redecorate the salon and he nearly always has the perfect thing!"

Carrie looked at Izzy, puzzled, wondering what her little sister was up to.

Izzy whispered to her, "I'll tell you later."

CHAPTER 6:

Bullies!

Mr Khan's was a curiosity shop filled with all sorts of ornaments, some new but mostly old. There were suits of armour and warrior helmets, along with ornamental table lamps with coloured glass shades. There were wall hangings with wonderful patterns: one was a huge map of the world knitted from different coloured wools, another was a rug of different shades of blue showing the solar system, with glass and ceramic spheres for the planets and sparkling beads for stars. Some of the things in the shop just looked lovely, and others were more useful or made beautiful musical sounds. Mum had decorated her beauty salon with a few antiques from Mr Khan's and she was always keen to see what new, interesting items he had in stock. Mr Khan was equally keen to show off the latest ornaments he'd been able to get his hands on.

"Mrs Clark!" he called with a smile as they entered the shop. "I was just thinking of you.

I've had a delivery of some beautiful rugs from Turkey that I think would be perfect for you! All pure wool and in lovely colours — would you like to take a look?"

Mum and Dad followed Mr Khan into the storeroom at the back while Izzy and Carrie stayed in the shop itself to look around. Izzy always liked coming to Mr Khan's. It was like a wonderful Aladdin's cave of treasures. And it was here that Izzy was sure she'd find what she was looking for.

"So why did you want to come here, Izzy?" asked Carrie.

"Because of what Dad said about Mrs Rice," she replied. "About her glass wind chimes that got broken. I'm sure Mr

Khan has wind chimes just like them, and I thought maybe we could get them as a present for Mrs Rice and cheer her up."

Carrie looked at her sister suspiciously. "What's brought this on all of a sudden?" she asked. "You don't usually do nice things for other people."

"Yes, I do!" protested Izzy. "It's just that no one notices when I do because of my clumsiness. I can't help having accidents sometimes."

"You spooked me with your ghost trick yesterday. That wasn't an accident, though, was it?" pointed out Carrie. Suddenly she stiffened. "Oh no!" she whispered, looking towards the door.

Izzy turned and saw an older boy and

girl who had just come into the shop. They had picked up some small glass paperweights with country scenes inside them and were throwing them to one another and giggling.

"Those are glass!" hissed Izzy to Carrie. She was horrified. "They could break them!"

She shot a look towards the door of the storeroom, where the adults were talking.

"We ought to go and tell Mr Khan," said Izzy.

"No," Carrie whispered back unhappily. "I know those two. Mike and Meryl Hibbert. They're twins in Year Nine at my school. They're really horrible bullies. Everyone's scared of them. If we tell Mr Khan, they'll tell everyone I'm a sneak. I don't want them to pick on me at school."

"But we have to do something!" said Izzy.

There *was* something she could try, but it meant breaking her promise to Mum and turning invisible. If she didn't, though, these bullies could wreck Mr Khan's stuff. And if she called for Mr Khan and told him what was going on, Carrie would get into trouble with the bullies. With a choice like that, which seemed like no choice at all, Izzy made her decision.

She pulled the feather out of her pocket and held it out to Carrie.

"Hide somewhere and look after this," she said.

Carrie took the feather and moved to hide behind a large rug on the wall as Izzy vanished.

The boy and girl were poking at some hanging ornaments now, as invisible Izzy crept up behind them.

"Hey, look," cackled Mike Hibbert. "These are just like those things we busted in that old lady's garden."

"Yeah," giggled his sister nastily. "That was fun!"

With a shock, Izzy realised that they were looking at wind chimes exactly the same as the decorations she'd seen hanging from the apple tree in Mrs Rice's front garden. It was Mike and Meryl who had wrecked Mrs Rice's garden!

Now there was even more reason for Izzy to give them a fright.

"Stop that!" Izzy whispered.

The boy swung round, an aggressive glare on his face. And then he gave a puzzled frown and looked around when he couldn't see anyone.

"Did you hear someone say something?" he asked his sister.

Meryl was looking around, too.

"I heard a voice," she said nervously. "But I can't see anyone."

"It was me," replied Izzy. "I am the ghost that haunts this shop!"

With that, Izzy reached out and picked up one of the wind chimes so that it seemed to float in mid-air.

"I know that you broke the decorations

in that lady's garden," she said. "I know every bad thing you've ever done, Mike and Meryl Hibbert!"

The boy looked towards Izzy, his eyes moving frantically left and right. The girl had gone pale.

"We must be imagining it," she said, not sounding very sure.

"We can't both be imagining the same thing at the same time," said the boy.

"It said it was a ghost," gulped Meryl. "It said it knew every bad thing we've ever done!"

Mike began to shake with fear.

"That's . . . that's what I heard!" he said, his teeth chattering.

Izzy put down the wind chime and picked up an old battered helmet from a suit of armour. She put it on her head, lifted the visor up so they could see the helmet was empty inside, then moved around menacingly in front of the pair.

"Do you promise to behave yourselves from now on?" hissed Izzy in her creepiest voice.

"Yes!" gulped Meryl, shaking.

"Yes!" echoed her brother, who looked like he was in a state of terror.

"Then go, and NEVER COME BACK HERE AGAIN!" yelled Izzy.

Mike gave a whimper and rushed out into the street, followed quickly by Meryl.

"That was brilliant!" said Carrie, coming out of her hiding place.

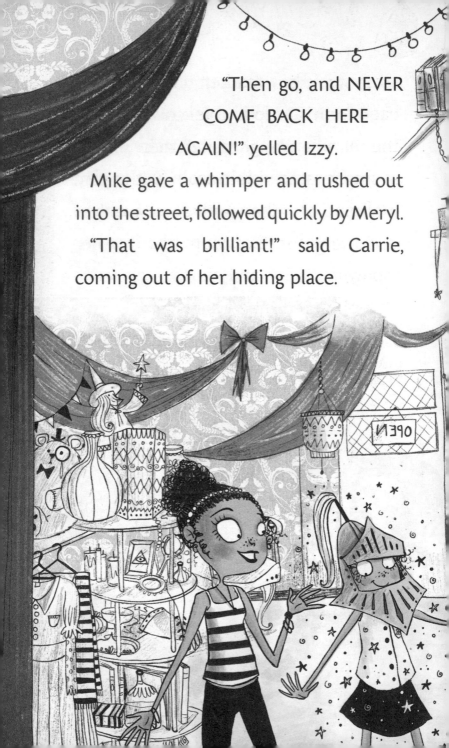

Izzy took her feather
back from Carrie and felt
the familiar tingling sensation
as she became visible again. But at that
moment Mr Khan walked out of the
storeroom ahead of Mum and Dad. His
mouth fell open and his eyes goggled as
he looked at her.

He's just seen me reappear, realised Izzy. *He saw the helmet floating about in the air, and then me appear in it!*

She took the helmet off and put it back on the shelf.

"Look at this, girls! This is perfect!" said Mum, coming towards them, holding up a small, brightly coloured rug. "Thank you, Mr Khan."

But the shopkeeper was still staring at Izzy, gobsmacked. He closed his mouth and rubbed his eyes with his hands, then opened them again.

"Are you all right, Mr Khan?" asked Dad. "You look like you've seen a ghost."

Carrie and Izzy looked at each other and did their best not to giggle.

"Er . . ." stammered Mr Khan.

Mum took some money out of her purse and paid Mr Khan for the rug.

"I know exactly where this will go in the salon," she said. "Thanks again. Right, girls, time for us to go. We'll drop you and your dad off at the park, Izzy, then Carrie and I are off to the boutique."

"Actually, Mum, I think I might like to go to the park after all," said Carrie.

Mum looked at her in surprise. "Are you sure?" she asked.

Carrie nodded. "It's been ages since me and Izzy played Frisbee." And she gave Izzy a smile.

Wow! thought Izzy, pleased. *Being invisible is making Carrie like me more!*

Mum shrugged. "Well, if that's what you want, that's fine by me. We can always do the boutique another time. Bye, Mr Khan!"

As they left the shop, Izzy could feel Mr Khan's bewildered, goggle-eyed stare still on her.

"Mr Khan saw me reappear," she whispered to Carrie.

"Don't worry about it," Carrie whispered back. She gave her little sister a hug. "You were brilliant in there, Izzy! I'm proud of you!"

CHAPTER 7:
Panic in the Park

It was a sunny day so there were quite a few people out in the park. It wasn't too busy, though, because it was also very windy, so there was plenty of space for Izzy and Carrie and Dad to play Frisbee. Eventually Mum joined in too, and even with sudden gusts of wind snatching the Frisbee high up into the air, they were soon having lots of fun. Mum and Carrie were the best, catching every throw neatly and sending the Frisbee on in a neat arc to the next person. Izzy wasn't bad, although she had to jump up now and then to catch the flying Frisbee, especially when Dad threw it. Dad also wasn't very good at catching. He dived to the left and missed it. He dived to the right and missed it.

And once when Mum passed the Frisbee to him in a perfect throw, a sudden gust of wind lifted it up so that it bounced off the top of his head and flew up into the air.

"Ow!" Dad called out loudly, before deliberately falling over and pretending to be knocked out.

Dad's antics made Izzy laugh so much that she fell over herself, rolling about on the grass with laughter. And as she did, the feather fell out of her pocket. She was having so much fun she didn't even notice the tingling sensation.

"Izzy!" yelled Carrie in alarm.

Izzy sat up, and when she saw the panicky look on the faces of Carrie, Mum and Dad, she realised that something terrible had happened. She saw the feather lying on the grass and reached out to pick it up, but before she could grab it, the wind blew it up into the air.

"No!" yelled Mum.

The whole family set off to chase after the feather, but it was no use and because Izzy was invisible Carrie kept running into her. The feather soared up into the air and disappeared over the tops of the trees.

Dad pulled out his mobile phone and frantically tapped Nana's number, then let out a big moan of disappointment. "I can't get a signal!" he groaned.

A flapping of wings and a squawk made them look up.

"Izzy!" squawked
Perky.

Perky landed
on Izzy, who
immediately
became visible
again. Perky dug into
his feathers with his beak and plucked
one out, which he offered to Izzy.

"Izzy!" he squawked again.

"Thank you, Perky!" said Izzy gratefully,
and she put the feather into her pocket,
making sure this time that it was secure.

"Yes, thank you, Perky!" repeated Mum,
and she stroked the parrot's feathers.

"How did Perky get here?" asked Dad,
puzzled. "I thought you were going to
leave him in your room, Izzy."

"I did," said Izzy. "He must have got out somehow."

"Squawk!" said Perky. "Perky fly!"

They heard a voice from behind the trees.

"Did you see that, Mum?"

A little boy was pointing at Izzy. His mum was sitting on the grass next to him, reading a magazine.

"That little girl vanished!" said the boy. "She was invisible. And then the parrot made her visible again!"

"Wayne, I've told you before about making up stories," said the boy's mother, not looking up from her magazine. "And a story about an invisible girl is *totally* unbelievable!"

CHAPTER 8
Izzy to the Rescue

Early the next morning, Dad was on the phone again to Nana Lin. This time, after he'd hung up, he told Izzy, Carrie and Mum, "She thinks she might have found the answer."

"Hurrah!" shouted Mum.

"She only *thinks* she might have," said Dad cautiously. "She's going to work on it today and run some tests. She hopes to have it sorted out by the end of school."

"What else did she say?" asked Izzy.

"Not a lot," said Dad. "Most of the time she was telling the dogs to shut up because they were barking every time something went bang. And there were a lot of bangs going on." He picked up his bag. "Right," he said. "I'm off to work. I'll see you all tonight, and fingers crossed you won't be Izzy the Invisible any more!"

After Dad left, Izzy thought about his words. No more invisibility. After what had happened at Mr Khan's shop, she was starting to think it could be fun, and useful. Perhaps she could persuade her mum to let her do it now and then?

"I'll pick you both up after school and take you to Nana's," said Mum. She gave Izzy a serious look. "Have you got that feather secure in your pocket, Izzy?"

"Yes, Mum," said Izzy, patting her blazer pocket. Mum had fixed the feather inside Izzy's pocket with a safety pin to make sure this one didn't accidentally fall out.

"You'd better go up and tell Perky you're off," said Mum. "We don't want him getting out and following you like he did yesterday."

"It was lucky he did," Carrie pointed out.

"Yes, it was," Mum admitted. "But I don't think the school would like it if Perky appears in Izzy's classroom!"

While Carrie packed her school bag, Izzy went upstairs to her room. Although the parrot could fly anywhere in the house, he'd chosen Izzy's room as his favourite place and spent most of his time in there. Carrie said it was because Izzy's room was so messy it must remind him of Nana Lin's house (which was a bit cheeky – but she might have been right).

Perky was perched on the chair by Izzy's dressing table and he flew to meet her as she came in, landing on her shoulder.

"I'm off to school, Perky," she told the parrot. "I wish you could come with me, but you can't. You have to stay here."

"Perky stay!" squawked the parrot. "Perky stay!"

"Good Perky," smiled Izzy. She stroked the parrot, who nuzzled her gently with his beak. "I'm so glad you came home with us," she told him. "I wonder if Nana will let you stay here with me after I'm not invisible any more?"

"Perky stay!" repeated the parrot, and he bounced up and down happily on Izzy's shoulder, flapping his wings.

"Izzy!" called Mum from downstairs. "Time to go!"

"Just coming, Mum!" Izzy shouted back. She stroked Perky one last time, and put him on his perch. "I'll see you when I get home. Bye, Perky!"

☆ ° ◎ ☆ ° ☆

As Izzy and Carrie walked towards the front gate, Carrie opened her bag and took out a sheet of paper, which she began to study.

"What's that?" Izzy asked.

"It's a chart I did for maths homework," said Carrie. "I've got to hand it in this morning. I'm just checking it's okay."

"The colours are pretty," said Izzy admiringly.

"It's a pie chart," said Carrie.

"You mean it's about pies?" asked Izzy.

"No," said Carrie, laughing at her little sister. "It's a kind of graph that shows you different amounts of things. Mine is about different sorts of shoes. I did a study of all the kids in my class, found out how many wear trainers, how many wear boots —"

Suddenly a gust of wind snatched the piece of paper from Carrie's fingers and blew it up into the air.

"No!" yelled Carrie in horror.

She reached for it but another gust of wind blew the paper over the fence into Mrs Rice's front garden.

"Oh no!" groaned Carrie.

"I saw that!" called a loud voice.

It was Mrs Rice. Her front door was

open and she had come rushing outside, looking rather angry. "I saw you throwing litter into my garden!" she said, looking at the girls.

"It's not litter," protested Carrie. "It's my maths homework. The wind blew it away!"

"Just like those vandals who made a mess of my garden!" carried on Mrs Rice, ignoring Carrie.

"I'm not at all like them!" appealed Carrie.

"It's true, Mrs Rice," added Izzy.

"Litter is supposed to go in a bin!" snapped the old lady angrily. And she picked up Carrie's homework, lifted the lid of her dustbin and dumped the piece of paper into it. "There!"

"But Mrs Rice . . ." begged Carrie.

"It's too late to apologise!" barked their neighbour. "I saw you throw it! Now get away with you. I shall be watching!"

With that, Mrs Rice went back inside and slammed the door. A moment later she appeared at the window and glared out at the two girls.

"I worked so hard on that chart," said Carrie, almost in tears. "If I don't hand it in I'll be in big trouble!"

"Leave it to me," said Izzy. "Come on."

The sisters walked round the corner, behind a tall hedge.

"Hold this," said Izzy, taking off her blazer and handing it to Carrie.

Then, invisible once more, Izzy walked up to Mrs Rice's gate, opened it and walked across to the dustbin. With a quick look around to make sure no one was watching, she lifted the lid, reached in and carefully took out Carrie's maths homework, then replaced the lid and hurried back.

Made it, thought Izzy, but as she closed the gate she saw Mrs Rice in the window, her eyes and mouth wide open in stunned astonishment, just as Mr Khan's had been.

Oh dear, thought Izzy. Still, there was no harm done. Maybe Mrs Rice would think the wind had lifted the lid off the dustbin and blown the piece of paper away . . . Surely she'd never think an invisible girl had been in her garden?

Izzy rejoined Carrie, handing her the pie chart and taking her blazer back.

"There!" she said.

Carrie looked at the pie chart, an expression of relief and delight on her face.

"Izzy, you are wonderful!" she said.

Izzy smiled. "Being invisible is cool!" she said. And she suddenly felt sad because it would soon be over.

CHAPTER 9

Being Nice to Mrs Rice

With Perky's feather firmly pinned inside her pocket, there were no more misadventures for Izzy. She didn't turn invisible even once at school. In fact, the only excitement came during break-time, when one of the boys pointed up and said excitedly, "Look! There's a parrot up there on the school roof!"

All the kids and the teachers on duty

looked up. Sure enough, there was Perky, perched on top of the roof. He had obviously opened the window again and followed Izzy to school, ready to come to her rescue if she needed it.

Perky, you are the nicest parrot in the world! Izzy thought to herself.

She waved, and with a friendly squawk Perky lifted up off the roof and flew towards some nearby trees. He was still going to be keeping an eye on her, but from the cover of the leafy branches. Like her very own guardian angel.

All day Izzy thought how if Nan's experiment worked she would no longer be able to turn invisible. On the one hand, she knew it would be a good thing, because keeping a feather on her at all times could be tricky. Going swimming would be particularly difficult! But, on the other hand, being invisible had meant she'd been able to do some really cool things, like get Carrie's precious homework back from Mrs Rice's dustbin, and stop those two bullies from messing with the ornaments in Mr Khan's shop.

When Carrie and Mum arrived in the car to collect Izzy from school, Izzy had made up her mind.

"Mum, before we go to Nana's, there's one more thing I need to do before I stop being invisible."

"What's that?" asked Mum.

"It's something for Mrs Rice," said Izzy. "To try to make her smile."

"You'll have a job making that happen,"

said Carrie doubtfully.

"But I'd like to try," said Izzy. "Please?"

"How are you going to do it?" asked Mum.

"I have an idea . . ." said Izzy. "Can we go back to Mr Khan's?"

☆。◎☆。☆

Inside Mr Khan's shop Izzy found just what she needed. But there was another reason she had wanted to return there. After Mum had paid for what they'd chosen she and Carrie headed for the door, but Izzy lagged behind a bit.

"Mr Khan," she began, "when you saw me appear out of thin air the other day, you weren't seeing things. I wasn't a ghost, I was just invisible, but I'm going to be all right now."

And then she hurried after her mum and sister, feeling much better because she'd told Mr Khan the truth and stopped him worrying that he might be seeing things.

Mr Khan stared after Izzy, his mouth

falling open again in shock, and he slumped down onto a chair in a state of bewilderment.

"Invisible!" he whispered to himself, a worried expression on his face. He shook his head. "Now I think people are *saying* odd things!"

CHAPTER 10:

Goodbye to Izzy the Invisible

Mum parked the car outside their house, and they all went indoors. Once they were in, Mum unpinned the feather from Izzy's pocket, and Izzy — now invisible — picked up her surprise and headed back outside.

Mrs Rice was by her window as usual, watching people passing by. She looked anxious, worried and suspicious.

After what happened to her garden, she doesn't trust people, thought Izzy. *Let's hope those horrible Hibbert twins have learned their lesson.*

Izzy opened the gate to Mrs Rice's front garden, and walked towards the apple tree.

Inside her house, Mrs Rice heard the sound of her gate opening and turned to the window, ready to shout angrily.

But she was astonished to see two beautiful wind chimes, just like the ones that had been damaged, floating through the air into her front garden. As she watched, the two ornaments hung themselves on the tree, and coloured ribbons wrapped around the branches to make the wind chimes secure.

Stunned, Mrs Rice came out into her garden and stood looking in wonder at the two lovely wind chimes dangling from the tree. As a slight breeze caught them they moved, and a musical sound tinkled out, like gentle fairy bells.

As Mrs Rice stood there, astonished, she didn't see her garden gate close and the latch click carefully into place.

Another slight gust of wind caught the

wind chimes, spinning them, making them turn and ring out their delicate tune, and Mrs Rice smiled, her whole face lighting up, her hands clasped together in joy.

"Thank you, whoever you are!" she whispered happily.

When Izzy got home, Perky flew down to her shoulder, making her reappear.

"It's lucky he didn't do that when you were in Mrs Rice's garden," said Carrie.

Izzy shook her head and stroked the parrot.

"He wouldn't have," she said. "He knew what I was doing."

"But he's a parrot," said Carrie. "How would he know?"

"Perky's always been my friend," said Izzy. "But since this all happened he and I have had a really special connection. For one thing, he's the only one who can see me when I'm invisible. And" – she smiled at Perky – "he's a parrot with a very good heart."

"And you are a lovely girl with a very good heart," said Mum. "You and Perky are two of a kind." She grinned and gave both girls a wink. "I think now is just the right time to celebrate."

"The cake?" asked Izzy hopefully.

"The cake," nodded Mum. "I can feel it calling us!"

☆ ◦ ◉ ✧ ◦ ✦

The cake was delicious! Carrie cut her chocolate half into neat slices, which she ate delicately, while Izzy munched away happily at the marzipan half, which left large blobs on her cheeks for her to wipe with her fingers and then lick them clean. For once, Mum didn't comment on Izzy's messy eating habits, or even when Izzy fed Perky bits of the cake.

Afterwards, when the cake was all gone and Izzy's face had been wiped, she sat in the living room with the parrot perched on her lap, stroking him sadly. Mum was outside, getting the car ready. It was time for Izzy to become properly visible again, which meant that Perky would be going back to Nana's house.

"I'm going to miss you, Perky," she said.

"Miss Izzy," said Perky.

She cuddled him to her. "Maybe Nana will let you stay with me," she said hopefully. But she knew that even if Nana agreed, Mum and Dad wouldn't.

Carrie put her head round the door.

"Mum says we're all ready to go, Izzy," she said. "It's time."

☆ ° ◎ ☆ ° ☆

Nana Lin greeted them with a broad smile as she opened the door. "I think I've found the cure!"

They followed her through to the kitchen, where all the animals had gathered: Griff and Gruff were sitting together on the floor, wagging their tails and looking excited. Itsy and Bitsy had joined Buddy up on the top shelf and all three cats were looking down on the scene in the kitchen with suspicious looks on their faces. Even Sid the snake had come out from the cover of his rocks to watch. Perky flew across the kitchen to a chair and perched on the back of it.

"We've had fun today," said Nana. "I've been making things disappear and reappear all day."

"The animals?" asked Izzy.

"No, no," said Nana. "That wouldn't be fair to them. No, I made a hat disappear, and come back again. And then I did it with a teapot. That's why the animals are all here, waiting to see what happens next." She picked up a bottle with yellow liquid inside it. "This is it!" she told them.

"What is it?" asked Mum.

"It's made from some of Perky's feathers," said Nana. "I worked out that they must hold the key to reversing the invisibility. And, because Perky's been moulting, I had a few of his feathers lying around."

"What do I do with it?" asked Izzy, looking at the liquid suspiciously.

"You spray it on," said Nana. "Like a perfume. It will get absorbed into your body immediately and sort everything out."

"Are you sure it will work?" asked Mum doubtfully.

"It worked with the hat and the teapot," said Nana. Then she gave a thoughtful frown. "Mind you, they're things, not people. I hope it'll work on Izzy but there's only one way to find out."

Nana picked up the perfume spray bottle.

So, this is it, Izzy thought. *If this works, I won't be able to become invisible ever again.*

It was strange — when it had first happened, Izzy had been scared. But then she'd started to get used to her invisibility. She'd been able to do good things with it, like stopping the bullies from messing up Mr Khan's shop, and hanging the wind chimes on Mrs Rice's apple tree and making her smile.

Perhaps I should tell Nana and Mum I don't want to use this stuff, she thought. *I want to be able to be invisible now and then.*

But when Izzy looked at the nervous expressions on the faces of Mum and Nana Lin, she realised how worried they were about her. They loved her and cared about her, and because of that they wanted her to be just the same as she was before. No longer invisible. And like Mum had said, there was the chance that one day Izzy might turn invisible and not be able to reappear, even with a feather from Perky.

Nana Lin handed the spray to Izzy. "Here," she said.

I have to do it, thought Izzy. *For them.*

Izzy took the bottle, aimed it at herself and pressed the button. She felt a mist of spray fall on her bare skin.

"There!" said Nana. "Now, put your feather aside, and we'll see what happens."

Izzy took the feather from her pocket and laid it carefully on the table. Nana, Mum and Carrie were all watching her closely.

"Well?" asked Izzy.

"We can still see you!" said Carrie.

"It worked!" said Nana delightedly, and she began to dance happily around the kitchen, causing the two dogs to leap up and join her, jumping around and barking excitedly. The three cats remained on the top shelf, looking down at Nana and the dogs in that superior way cats do, while Perky added to the excitement by flying around the kitchen, looping the loop and squawking happily. Mum, Carrie and Izzy danced joyfully below him, hugging and skipping. When they had all calmed down, Perky settled back on his perch.

"Well done!" said Mum with a sigh of relief. "Now we can get back to living our normal life again!"

Izzy scooped the parrot up in her arms, hugging him gratefully.

"Thank you, Perky," she said. Then she whispered, "You saved me when I was invisible, and you've saved me again now! I'm going to miss having you around the house."

Nana was smiling. "But you know you can come and see him any time you want to, Izzy."

"Providing you don't get involved in any more of Nana's experiments!" said Mum firmly.

"I promise," said Izzy, smiling shyly.

She put Perky back on his perch and stroked his feathers.

"Thank you, Perky," she whispered. "I'll come and see you tomorrow."

☆ ∘ ⊚ ☆ ∘ ☆

Dad was waiting in the hallway when they got home.

"I came home from work early," he said. "What happened? Did Nana find the cure for you?"

"Show him, Izzy," smiled Mum.

Izzy stepped forwards and let Perky's feather fall to the floor. "Look, Dad – no Perky, and no feather," grinned Izzy. "I'm back to normal."

"What a relief!" sighed Dad. "I've been so worried all day! And on top of that the plumbing at the gym went wrong again . . ."

As Dad began to tell Mum about his day, Carrie gestured to Izzy. "I've got something to show you," she said.

Curious, Izzy followed her sister upstairs.

Inside Carrie's room, Carrie opened her drawer and took out her diary.

"You asked me the other day if I'd written anything about you in my diary," she said, untying the ribbon that was around it. "Well, I did."

Carrie opened the diary and showed it to Izzy. There was a drawing of Izzy with the words IZZY THE INVISIBLE, and beneath it Carrie had written: My little sister, Izzy, is brilliant. She is a Superhero. She scores Top Marks for being brave and being kind. If she wasn't clumsy and messy, she'd be almost perfect. She is the best sister there is.

Touched, Izzy hugged her big sister really tight.

"No," said Izzy. "*You're* the best sister there is."

"Let's not argue," smiled Carrie. "We're *both* the best sisters."

And Carrie squeezed Izzy back even tighter, causing Izzy to hiccup . . . and vanish.

"Oh no!" said Carrie. Looking shocked, she stepped back from her invisible little sister. "The cure didn't work!"

But then Izzy reappeared, as solid and real as ever.

"Yes it did," said Izzy. "There must have been just a little bit of invisibility left over. That's the end of it now."

At least, she thought, *I* think *that's the end of it . . .*

LOUISE GRAY loves dancing, fairies and the miracles of nature, especially the magic of woods. When she was small she wanted to be a cowboy. Not a cow*girl*, but a cowboy, riding the range. Unfortunately there wasn't much vast prairie in the part of Kent where she grew up, so instead she lived in a fantastic country called Her Imagination, where she still lives today.

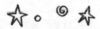

LAURA ELLEN ANDERSON attended her local school of Witchcraft and Wizardry before deciding to become an author/illustrator. She is the creator of *Evil Emperor Penguin* and artist for many other books including the Witch Wars series, *Snowflakes* and *Harper and the Scarlet Umbrella*. When she's not writing and illustrating, Laura practises her invisibility and riding her pet dragon. Follow Laura at www.lauraellenanderson.co.uk or on Twitter: @Lillustrator.

The purrfect series for
animal lovers and young readers

QUEEN
SARDINE

Ivy's best friend is a cat.
It's true. But Queen Sardine is no
ordinary kitty - and Ivy
can understand every
word she says!

Twins Eddie and Izzie are
very surprised when the school
lizard they're looking after
starts breathing fire!

They're going to need the help of . . .

The Secret Animal Society

Exciting, mythical creatures
and adventures galore!